ALL
FOR THE BEST!

Hans Wilhelm

for the evolving human spirit

HAMPTON ROADS
PUBLISHING COMPANY, INC.

Cover art and illustrations by Hans Wilhelm

Hampton Roads Publishing Company, Inc.
1125 Stoney Ridge Road
Charlottesville, VA 22902

434-296-2772
fax: 434-296-5096
e-mail: hrpc@hrpub.com
www.hrpub.com

If you are unable to order this book from your local
bookseller, you may order directly from the publisher.
Call 1-800-766-8009, toll-free.

Library of Congress Cataloging-in-Publication Data

Wilhelm, Hans.
    All for the best / Hans Wilhelm.
       p. cm.
    Summary: Though the villagers do not understand his attitude,
  an old carpet weaver is not upset when bad things happen to
  him nor is he elated when he has good fortune.
    ISBN 1-57174-344-8 (hardcover : alk. paper)
    [1. Optimism--Folklore. 2. Folklore.]   I. Title.
  PZ8.1.W6445Al 2003
  398.22--dc21
  [E]
                                    2002013093

10 9 8 7 6 5 4 3 2 1

Printed on acid-free paper in China

The wise master
learns to meet the
changing circumstances of life
with an equitable spirit
neither elated by success
nor depressed by failure.

—Buddha

In the rugged hills of the land of dawn there lived a carpet weaver.

His skills were well known, for his carpets were treasured all over the province. Their colors were deep and rich like precious jewels, and their designs had the radiance of the morning sun.

Day after day as the carpet weaver quietly worked at his loom, his grandson tended the sheep.

One moonless night a bandit entered the field of the carpet weaver and stole one of his sheep.

When the news of the crime reached his neighbors, they rushed to the home of the carpet weaver.

Their voices were filled with rage, "We must catch the thief! He must be punished!"

But the carpet weaver kept on weaving and quietly said, "It will be for the best."

Puzzled and perplexed, the neighbors withdrew.

The next day the bandit was caught. The judge ordered him to return the stolen sheep and to also give his horse to the carpet weaver as penance. And a fine horse it was!

Pleased that justice had ruled, the neighbors came to the weaver's home to celebrate.

"You're a lucky man!" they cheered, "The winds of good fortune are with you."

But the weaver kept on weaving, and he quietly said, "It will be for the best."

Soon after, the horse broke out
of the paddock and ran away.

The neighbors again came to comfort the carpet weaver. They raised their voices, bemoaning his loss.

"Oh, dear friend, what a terrible misfortune!" they lamented.

But the carpet weaver kept on weaving and quietly said, "It will be for the best."

Startled and confused, the neighbors shook their heads and left.

A few days later the weaver's horse
returned—followed by two wild horses.

Now the carpet weaver had three
horses instead of one.

The neighbors came to rejoice in his good
fortune. They congratulated him and told
him how lucky he was.

But the carpet weaver kept on weaving,
and he quietly said, "It will be for the best."

A few days later, the weaver's grandson
attempted to break in one of the wild horses.
It bucked and kicked and threw him off.
He fell to the ground and broke his leg.

Once again the neighbors
came to commiserate. "Oh,
what terrible luck!" they cried
and pitied him.

But the carpet weaver kept on
weaving, and he quietly said,
"It will be for the best."

This time the neighbors were
enraged by his reply. Was he
mocking their words of
sympathy? Had he no feelings
for his grandchild? Or had he
simply gone crazy?

Whatever it was, they decided
that they no longer wanted to
have anything to do with him.

The next day, the king came through the
village looking for soldiers for his war.

Loud were the cries of mothers, wives, and children as
every able-bodied man and boy in the village was taken.

Every able-bodied man—but not the carpet weaver's grandson.

"Grandfather," said the boy as he helped cut the huge carpet from the loom, "Why do you always say 'It will be for the best,' even when bad things happen?"

The weaver spread the carpet out on the ground, and then he said, "I will tell you a secret: I always see and expect the best—even in my darkest hour."

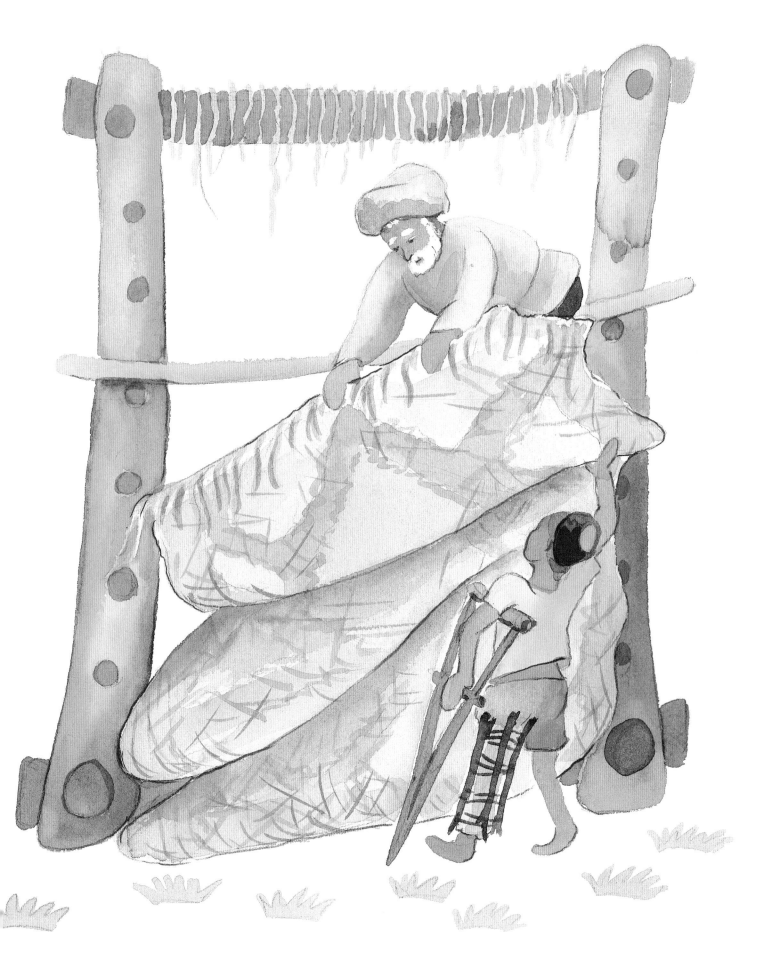

"We seldom know the reason why good
or bad things happen to us," he said.

"Life is like the wrong side of a carpet.
We see many different colored threads
running every which way. They seem
to make no sense at all.

"But one day," he continued, as he turned
the carpet over, "in this life or thereafter . . .

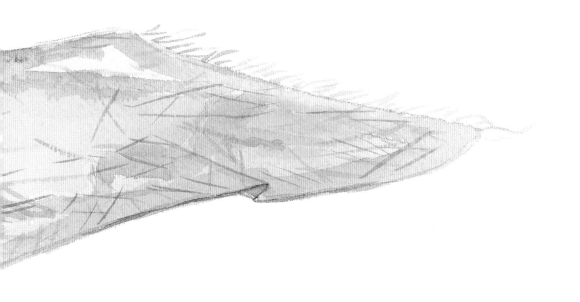

. . . we will see the right side of the carpet,
and then we will realize that it has all made
a perfect pattern!"

And so it has.

 Hampton Roads Publishing Company is dedicated to providing quality children's books that stimulate the intellect, teach valuable lessons, and allow our children's spirits to grow. We have created our line of Young Spirit Books for the evolving human spirit of our children. Give your children Young Spirit Books—their key to a whole new world!

Hampton Roads Publishing Company
publishes books on a variety of subjects including
metaphysics, health, complementary medicine,
visionary fiction, and other related topics.

For a copy of our latest catalog,
call toll-free, 800-766-8009,
or send your name and address to:

Hampton Roads Publishing Company, Inc.
1125 Stoney Ridge Road
Charlottesville, VA 22902
e-mail: hrpc@hrpub.com
www.hrpub.com